PROTECTING ANIMALS

BY DARLENE R. STILLE

Published by The Child's World®
1980 Lookout Drive • Mankato, MN 56003-1705
800-599-READ • www.childsworld.com

PHOTO CREDITS
Michelle D. Milliman/Shutterstock Images, cover, 1; Peter Pattavina/
iStockphoto, 5; Larisa Lofitskaya/Shutterstock Images, 7; Dmitry
Deshevykh/iStockphoto, 9; Marcio Jose Bastos Silva/Shutterstock
Images, 11; Lee Feldstein/iStockphoto, 13; Paul Tessier/iStockphoto, 15;
Morgan Lane Photography/Shutterstock Images, 17; Aldo Murillo/
iStockphoto, 19; Shutterstock Images, 21, 23; Tom Abraham/
iStockphoto, 25; Stéphane Bidouze/Shutterstock Images, 27; Simone
van den Berg/Shutterstock Images, 29

CONTENT CONSULTANT
Mark C. Andersen, professor of fish, wildlife, and conservation ecology,
New Mexico State University

ACKNOWLEDGMENTS
The Child's World®: Mary Berendes, Publishing Director
The Design Lab: Design
Red Line Editorial: Editorial direction

ISBN: 978-1-60973-174-8
LCCN: 2011927673

Printed in the United States of America in Mankato, MN
July, 2011
PA02090

TABLE OF CONTENTS

ANIMALS IN DANGER

Wrapped in a coat of beautiful white fur, the Arctic fox roams over the ice and snow of the Arctic. Every year, however, there is less Arctic ice and snow. The cold home of the Arctic fox is melting away. The loss of **habitat** is a main reason an animal becomes **endangered**. What causes a loss of habitat?

One cause is **global warming**. Gases from cars, power plants, and factories rise in the **atmosphere**. The gases trap too much heat from the sun. The trapped heat melts the ice and snow where Arctic animals live.

Nonnative species contribute to loss of habitat, too. Nonnative species are animals

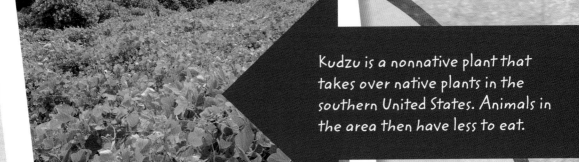

Kudzu is a nonnative plant that takes over native plants in the southern United States. Animals in the area then have less to eat.

and plants that are living outside the places they normally live or grow. People usually bring nonnative species to an area. The nonnative species compete with **native** species for food and space to live. A nonnative plant may take over a plant that was eaten by a native animal. The animal then has less food to survive.

There is still time to save endangered animals. See what you can do to help protect them!

DON'T WEAR REAL FUR

Check labels on coats and other clothing to make sure any fur on them is fake. If it's real, the fur might be from an endangered animal. Tell your parents and other grown-ups that it's not cool to buy or wear fur.

WHY?

It is against the law in many countries to hunt endangered animals. It is also against the law to bring the skin or any other part of an endangered animal into the United States. **Poachers** break these laws. They trap and shoot endangered animals. They try to sell the skins to smugglers who bring them into the United States. If people stop buying the furs, the poachers will go out of business.

Before you get a new winter coat or hat that has fur, make sure the fur is fake.

ADOPT AN ANIMAL IN DANGER

Adopt an animal from the World Wildlife Fund or Defenders of Wildlife. An Arctic fox from Defenders of Wildlife costs about $15. A tiger from the World Wildlife Fund costs about $25. You don't get to keep the animal, but you do help it. These groups use the money to help fight for laws that protect animals.

WHY?

There are endangered animals in every animal group. More frogs and other amphibians are in danger of dying out than animals of any other group. About 20 percent of mammals are in danger and about 10 percent of birds. Even some types of fish are in danger. Overfishing, or catching too many of one kind of fish, causes this problem.

Money donated to Defenders of Wildlife helps protect the habitats of Arctic foxes.

KICKING IN FOR KAKAPO

Thirteen-year-old Aaron Friedman of Connecticut is helping to save an endangered parrot. Aaron learned the kakapo are the world's rarest and largest parrots. They live in New Zealand, and they cannot fly. He also learned they are endangered and wanted to help them. Aaron had a request for the guests at his bar mitzvah. He asked them to donate money to the Kakapo Recovery Programme in New Zealand. Aaron's gifts raised $2,500 to help the parrots.

TIP #3

PLANT A BUTTERFLY HABITAT

Find out what butterflies live in your area. Then find out what flowers they like. Plant those flowers in your backyard. Watch the butterflies flutter into their new home. Pull weeds and other plants if they start to grow so only plants the butterflies like will be in the garden.

WHY?

Many butterflies get their food, nectar, from flowers. And most butterfly species only like one kind of flower. Nonnative species can come into an area and take over the plants butterflies like. Then the butterflies will have no food.

Flowers provide food for many butterflies.

DON'T KEEP ENDANGERED PETS

Many snakes and parrots are endangered because too many were caught and sold as pets. Endangered pets include the San Francisco garter snake and the Amazon parrot. These animals are caught and sold illegally. Taking these animals from their habitats further endangers them.

WHY?

If no one wants to own an endangered pet, the people who illegally catch and sell them will no longer make money. They will soon go out of business and stop catching the animals.

Endangered animals such as the Amazon parrot should not be kept as pets.

LEARN WHAT WORKS

Have any endangered animals been saved?
Yes they have. The bald eagle and grizzly bear
are no longer on the endangered species list.
How did this happen? Do some research to find
out. Go to the library or search on the Internet.
Maybe you can help get another animal off the
endangered species list.

WHY?

Three kinds of efforts saved the American
alligator. Lawmakers passed laws that protect
alligators from hunters. Measures were passed
to protect the alligators' swampy habitats. And
laws made it illegal to sell shoes, belts, purses,
and other items made from alligator skin.

The grizzly bear is no longer an endangered species.

RAISE MONEY

Raise money to donate to your favorite **conservation** group. Set up a lemonade stand. Gather some friends and have a bake sale. Grown-ups can help you make cookies or brownies. Make a sign telling customers their money will help animals in need.

WHY?

The biggest conservation group is the World Wildlife Fund. It runs about 1,300 projects all around the world. It needs about $150 million a year to keep these programs running. Every little bit helps!

You and your friends can have a lemonade stand to raise money that will help protect animals.

TIP #7

WRITE A LETTER

Let others know you believe protecting animals is important. Write a letter to the editor of your local paper. Explain why endangered animals need to be saved. Write a letter to your local or national lawmakers. Ask them to pass laws that protect animals.

WHY?

Telling lawmakers how you feel is important. You're not old enough to vote. But you are old enough to be heard by Congress members. They should take your concerns seriously.

Write a letter asking your Congress member to pass laws that will help protect animals and their habitats.

START A PETITION

Petitions let lawmakers know that many people feel a certain way. Your petition might say that the government needs to help get rid of nonnative species in your area. You sign the petition. You then ask your friends and neighbors to sign. Then send the petition to one of your lawmakers.

WHY?

Lawmakers need to know that many people want animals to be saved. Being as specific as possible helps. Let them know the field behind your house has nonnative plants that may cause trouble for animals. The more people who sign the petition, the better the chance that laws helping animals will get passed.

Ask people to sign your petition in order to help protect animals.

TIP #9

WALK OR RIDE
YOUR BIKE

Instead of asking your parents to drive you somewhere, walk. If it is too far to walk, ride your bike. Your actions help protect nature and animals.

WHY?

Most cars burn gasoline. This contributes to global warming. Global warming causes ice at the poles to melt. When this ice melts, polar bears have a harder time finding food. They are starting to die out. Using less gas means less global warming, and more ice for the polar bears!

Riding your bike can help stop global warming and the loss of many animals' habitats.

HELPING ENDANGERED APES

What can an elementary student do? Ask Haley Stern of Vermont. She fell in love with the gorillas at the Bronx Zoo in New York. She learned that these amazing animals are endangered. At age ten, she started a group called Kids Save Apes. The group helps raise money to save these endangered animals.

CUT OFF VAMPIRE ENERGY

When you hit the *OFF* button on the television remote control, the screen goes blank. Still, the television uses energy. Many electronics use energy when they are turned off. These include televisions, computers, and microwaves. The energy used is called vampire energy. You can stop this energy waste by unplugging electronics after you turn them off.

WHY?

Vampire energy loss costs about $4 billion each year in the United States. A lot of electricity comes from power plants that burn fossil fuels and give off carbon dioxide gas. Too much of this gas in Earth's atmosphere contributes to global warming.

Unplug electronics
to help save
electricity and the
habitats of animals.

SPREAD THE WORD

Help teach people about the importance of saving endangered animals. Get a group of friends to set up a table in a mall or at a fair. Ask conservation groups to send some fliers for you to hand out. Or, you can make your own. Explain how saving endangered animals helps preserve the **biodiversity** of life on Earth. An area is rich in biodiversity when it has many animals, plants, and other living things.

WHY?

Protecting biodiversity is important to keep Earth healthy. The more species there are, the better an environment can recover from a natural disaster.

Rain forests are some of the most biodiverse places on Earth. They need to be protected for the many animals that live in them.

GET INVOLVED

Join a conservation group near your home. If there isn't one, you can join the National Zoo's Conservation Kids' Club online. Learn about the zoo's animals, especially the endangered golden lion tamarin. Chat online with experts. Learn about programs to save other endangered animals.

WHY?

By joining a conservation group such as the World Wildlife Fund, Nature Conservancy, or the Sierra Club, you can have a real impact on protecting animals. Some of these groups have smaller local or state groups. You can volunteer with them to make a difference.

Volunteer at an aquarium or zoo to learn more about animals and how to help protect them.

MORE WAYS TO GO GREEN

1. **Do** you have a birthday coming up? Instead of getting gifts, ask friends and family to donate the money they were going to spend on your gift to a conservation group.

2. **Volunteer** at a local zoo or aquarium to learn about animals in person.

3. **Ask** your parents to use smart plug strips. These power strips can sense when a device is not in use and stop its use of vampire energy.

4. **Unplug** your cell phone charger when your cell phone has finished charging.

5. **Ask** the adults in your home to always buy Energy Star appliances, which use less vampire energy.

6. **Talk** to your teacher to see if your class can raise money to adopt an endangered animal.

7. **Put** on a sweater instead of turning up the thermostat when it is cold. By saving on home heating, you help reduce the burning of fossil fuels that leads to global warming.

8. **Turn** off the lights when you leave a room. This reduces energy use and greenhouse gases.

9. **Start** a nature journal. List and draw all the animals you can find in a nearby park. Do research to make sure they are all native.

10. **Make** a poster about an endangered animal and put it in your window.

11. **Donate** your used toys to an organization that will recycle them, such as Goodwill Industries or the Salvation Army. Go to these places when you are looking for a new toy to play with. Making toys in factories takes energy and that energy usually comes from fossil fuels.

12. **Close** the doors to your house to save energy in summer when the air conditioner is running and in winter when the heat is on.

atmosphere (AT-muss-feer): The atmosphere is the layer of gases around Earth. Pollution has a negative impact on the atmosphere.

biodiversity (by-oh-duh-VURS-it-ee): Biodiversity is the condition in nature where a wide variety of living things live in a single area. Protecting biodiversity on Earth also protects animals.

conservation (kon-sur-VAY-shun): Conservation is the preservation of the natural world. Conservation is important to keep all animals healthy and living on Earth.

endangered (en-DAYN-jurd): If something is endangered, it is in danger of dying out. It is important to protect endangered animals and help their numbers grow.

global warming (GLOHB-ul WOR-ming): Global warming is the heating up of Earth's atmosphere and oceans due to air pollution. Global warming affects the habitats of animals.

habitat (HAB-uh-tat): A habitat is the natural home of an animal or other living thing. An animal may become endangered if its habitat is lost.

native (NAY-tiv): If something is native, it is belonging to a certain place. Native animals may be harmed if nonnative species take over.

nonnative (NON-nay-tiv): If something is nonnative, it is in a place different from where it is originally from. A nonnative plant can take over a native plant's habitat.

poachers (POHCH-urz): Poachers are people who take or kill wild animals illegally. Poachers contribute to animals being endangered.

FURTHER READING

BOOKS

Edwards, Robert. *Polar Bears: In Danger.*
New York: Grosset & Dunlap, 2008.

George, Jean Craighead. *The Buffalo Are Back.*
New York: Dutton Juvenile, 2010.

Haywood, Karen. *Crocodiles and Alligators (Endangered!).*
Tarrytown, NY: Marshall Cavendish, 2010.

WEB SITES

Visit our Web site for links about protecting animals:
http://www.childsworld.com/links

Note to Parents, Teachers, and Librarians: We routinely verify our Web links to make sure they are safe and active sites. So encourage your readers to check them out!

INDEX